John Robertson Nicoll

THE BALLOON MAN IN APRIL
A TALE OF EDINBURGH IN SPRING

First published in paperback by
Michael Terence Publishing in 2024
www.mtp.agency

Copyright © 2024 John Robertson Nicoll

John Robertson Nicoll has asserted the right to be identified
as the author of this work in accordance with the
Copyright, Designs and Patents Act 1988

ISBN 9781800947740

All characters and events in this publication,
other than those in the public domain, are fictitious,
and any resemblance to real persons, is purely coincidental

All rights reserved. No part of this publication may be reproduced,
stored in a retrieval system, or transmitted,
in any form or by any means, electronic, mechanical,
photocopying, recording or otherwise,
without the prior permission of the publisher

Illustrated by
Harriet Buckley

Cover design
Copyright © 2024 Michael Terence Publishing

Michael Terence
Publishing

For My Mother and Father

April,

Comes like an idiot,

babbling and strewing flowers.

- Spring by Edna St. Vincent Millais

CONTENTS

1: FRIDAY ... AND A NEW ARRIVAL 1
2: A MEETING 8
3: SATURDAY ... AND THE SUN IS SHINING ... 16
4: DRISCOLL RISES 21
5: FEEDING THE INNER MAN 26
6: THE HOUR OF GLORY APPROACHES 30
7: THE RACE IS RUN 33
8: THE EVENING'S VELVET EMBRACE 38
9: THE GHOST OF A SMILE 45
10: A BRIEF BUT TENDER HAUNTING 51
11: ALL THE WARMTH OF THE PAST VISITS THE UNWORTHY DRISCOLL 59
12: SUNDAY MORNING ECHOES OF THE NIGHT BEFORE 63
13: TEA AND EMPATHY 66
14: LOVED AND UNLOVED 72
15: THE HIGH PRICE OF CHIPS 79
16: THE SCATTERING WINDS OF SPRING 90

1
FRIDAY ... AND A NEW ARRIVAL

Edinburgh – some years ago ...

Until then, April had not been kind to Edinburgh. The weather had been squally, wet and cold and a perpetual air of greyness had hung over the City like some sadness that refused to be forgotten. Then, on the second Friday of the month, everything changed. In the morning a series of light showers blew across the City and out over the North Sea and shortly after lunchtime the sun started to grow in strength and billowy, cotton wool clouds sailed at a brisk pace across what was now an otherwise blue sky.

Light and colour animated Auld Reekie. Church spires glinted, the polished domes of the public buildings gleamed and the shop windows along Princes Street shone as if drawing attention to the wonders of the goods displayed inside and the grass in the Gardens across the road positively glowed in the belated Spring sunshine.

The people making their way home looked as shocked and dazed as small animals pulled abruptly from their winter hibernation. They sat with friends in coffee shops or stood impatiently at bus stops, fervently hoping that this fine day marked the end of a particularly hard Edinburgh winter. A few optimistic souls even dared to think further ahead to warm, carefree Summer days and mild evenings when they would no longer have any need to brace themselves against those cutting winds that swept in from the North Sea.

FRIDAY ... AND A NEW ARRIVAL

There was, however, one soul, now just arriving in the city, who had no notion of how cold it could be. He had seen the blue sky and the fleecy clouds and the sunshine from a distance and, as we all know, distance lends enchantment.

Buster, being a simple soul who always wanted to believe the best of people and places, had convinced himself that the place that lay beneath that patch of sky must indeed be enchanted. You and I may laugh, cynical beings that we are, but Buster was always ready to embrace new wonders. Accordingly, he was the first one off the train when it arrived in the station. Breathless with excitement, he scrambled down on to the platform, picked up his battered suitcase and headed off in the direction of the main concourse.

Once there, he stopped dead in his tracks, sweating and confused. At a loss as to what to do now, he stood watching the destinations change on the main notice board while passers by gave the little man with the bulging eyes the widest of berths. He was oblivious to their stares, though, as the notice board seemed to have a hypnotic effect on him. Then, just above his head, a tannoy burst into loud, metallic life.

"16.44 for Aberdeen calling at Haymarket, Inverkeithing, Aberdour" ... He read all the names leading up to that great northern city, rolling them around his mouth with nearly as much pleasure as he derived from sucking boiled sweets. "Kinghorn, Kirkcaldy, Markinch" ... but, after a while he grew tired of the novelty and turned to seek directions.

A passing business woman, alarmed by his anxious, bulging eyes brushed him aside with her briefcase and carried on her way without breaking her stride.

FRIDAY ... AND A NEW ARRIVAL

Then he approached a South American tourist who was only too willing to help but did not seem to have as much as six words of English to his name.

Two youths in football shirts only laughed and swore loudly and made threatening gestures as they passed him by.

The minutes on the station clock ticked relentlessly by and the little man began to feel the sting of panic in the pit of his stomach. Every rejection only served to fuel his panic and he began to fear that he might never get past the station's exit.

As he turned this way and that, at the sound of every approaching footstep, a collective buzz seemed to pass through the station concourse like some invisible electric current and travellers, according to their nature, felt varying degrees of pity, embarrassment or irritation – but none of them stopped to help.

Eventually, a police man approached. At the sound of the officer's voice behind him, Buster wheeled round and immediately launched into a rambling attempt to explain his predicament but, when he realised who he was talking to, fell silent, lowered his gaze and stared for a long moment at his cracked, leather boots. Buster did not like uniforms. Uniforms, in his experience, usually meant a "ticking off", a "moving on" or worse.

P.C. Ernie Blyth examined this "specimen" for a moment while he pondered the best course of action. He had always thought that there was definitely "something in the air" where railway stations were concerned. If you stood in one place long enough you could bet that, sooner or later, every derelict, crank or plain nutcase would end up

FRIDAY ... AND A NEW ARRIVAL

in your lap. A Transport Policeman's lot was seldom a happy one!

The constable wondered which one of the above categories this wee bauchle fell into and, for his part, Buster affected the usual ingratiating smile that he always employed in these circumstances and when that failed to have any noticeable effect on the officer's stony countenance, he fell to contemplating his boots again.

P.C. Blyth had made his diagnosis by now. "Nutcase, pure and simple!" You only had to look at the way the big boogly eyes moved back and forth and up and down to see that. He was sure that this unfortunate wee craitur had escaped from some institution or another. In any event he was bound to be on someone's wanted list.

On the other hand, Blyth rationalised, he was not the world's keeper ... and the paperwork ... and besides, you could not take a citizen into custody just because they were stupid, fat and ugly. And he seemed a harmless enough wee bugger anyway but, finally, by way of paying lip service to proper procedure, the constable asked Buster to show some proof of means of support.

Buster thought for a moment before fishing out a Building Society Passbook from his jacket pocket. The P.C. examined the current balance with barely concealed envy before brushing Buster and his Passbook away.

Less than five minutes later, Buster was standing at the eastern end of Princes Street Gardens. His long journey and the panic in the train station were only memories now and so he raised his face to the Spring sky and said a silent "thank you" to his Maker for a safe arrival. Then,

FRIDAY ... AND A NEW ARRIVAL

remembering his purpose, he opened the cardboard suitcase and rummaged around for his "gifts".

It was the start of a fine April evening and the old man felt better than he could remember feeling in a very long time. Mind you it was something of an effort to feel better at his age but when Mother Nature was making such an effort herself, what with all the greenery and little creatures running hither and thither and suchlike, it would have been churlish not to at least try to feel well.

He sat down on his favourite bench, opened his Thermos flask and surveyed the Gardens as he sipped, birdlike, at the hot coffee and remembered what Spring had meant to him when he was a young man.

He remembered again the wonder of all life's possibilities that had only lain sleeping under the dead hand of winter and the way that, once the last chill of winter had gone Spring breezes always teased you with whispers of fine days ahead and holidays and girls in summer dresses. Now, at his age he would have thought that thoughts of that kind would not matter any more ... but, oh, how they did!

Why, he wondered, did the Spring tantalise him by bringing life and hope back to his tired old body. What was the use of it? Would it not be better employed bestowing its gifts elsewhere?

There were two of the creatures, one of which was now on the ground a few feet away. It thrust out its head and neck as it studied the little man in half mast trousers and shabby raincoat. It sniffed the air. It turned its head to one side as if waiting for an assurance of safety from some Guardian

FRIDAY ... AND A NEW ARRIVAL

Spirit in the Spring breeze. It edged closer, sniffing and twitching. As Buster wheezily crooned encouragement it came closer and closer still. When the squirrel was no more than a foot away from him it froze, one paw stretched before it, like a gun dog in a sporting print. Buster was about to offer more encouragement but then thought better of it, being content to stifle his wheezing lest the little creature lost its nerve at the last moment.

Then, with a lightning dart, the squirrel claimed its trophy from Buster's outstretched hand and ran off to a safe distance from where it sat on its hind legs attacking the nut with manic concentration. Buster was hoping that it would come for another treat but, for no good reason that he could see, the creature turned tail, scampered across the grass and up the trunk of the furthest away of two sycamore trees.

After a few moments Buster waddled over to the nearest of the two trees. From a branch eight feet from the ground a second squirrel glared down at him. Like its mate before, it inched forward but, this time, with an air of menace and it chattered hysterically as Buster fished in his pocket for more nuts. He held out two of them in the palm of his hand and stood as still as he could but the waves of hostility from the small inhabitant of that tree meant that even a patient soul like Buster had to admit defeat. He shrugged his shoulders in resignation and, with no ill will whatsoever, walked back to collect his case.

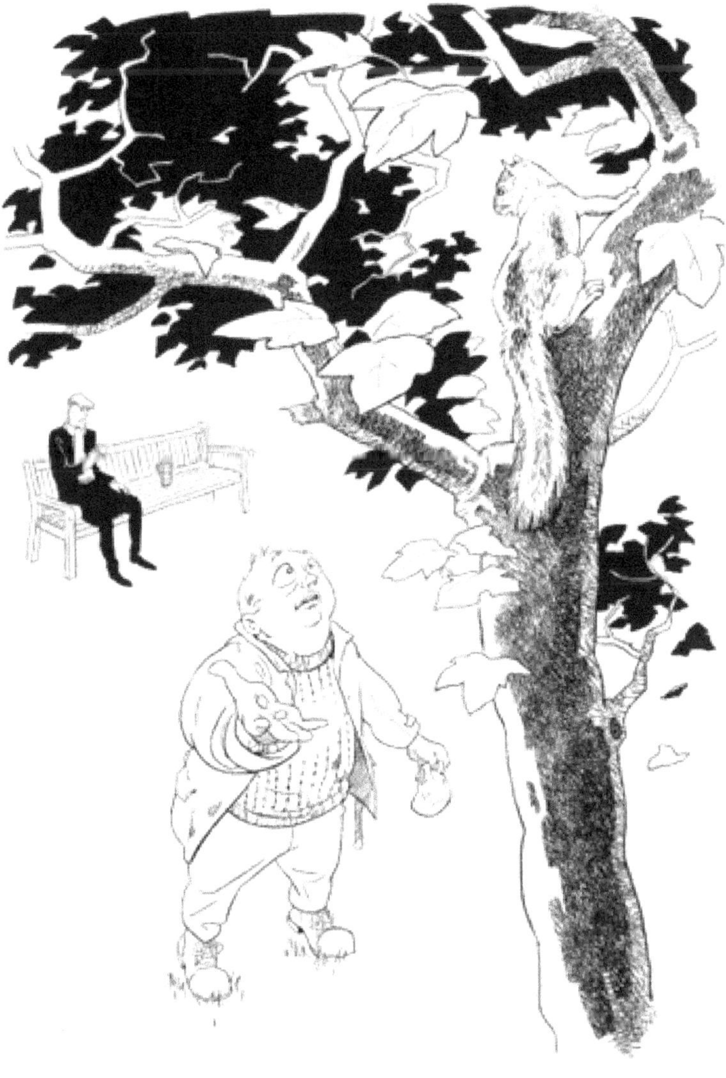

2
A MEETING

His first sight of the old man made him start in surprise, but Josef, seeing the look of alarm on Buster's face, raised his arm in greeting and reassurance and nodded to the trees and their small inhabitants, quoting an apposite Polish proverb. Then, remembering himself, he provided a halting English translation.

When the penny finally dropped Buster grinned broadly. Eager to make a new friend in a strange city, he lunged forward and gripped the old man's hand, pumping it vigorously. Josef winced and tried as diplomatically as he could to free his arthritic hand from the little man's grip.

The old landlord's new acquaintance jabbered excitedly as he picked up his suitcase, giving a blow by blow account of the course that his life had taken over the last few days. In a deluge of words he described his first impressions of the city that he had seen for the first time a mere hour ago and only when the flood of words subsided did he stop for breath before mentioning how hungry he was, and how tired, and his worries about where he would lay his head for the night.

Josef opened his mouth but, before he could speak, Buster, who felt that it was a formal requirement when making a new acquaintance, now took it upon himself to recite his entire life story from the moment of his birth to this very minute but Josef's mind was preoccupied with certain pressing questions – chief among them being what on earth was he supposed to do with this strange little creature, who for all the world could have sprung from some children's story in which elves and goblins featured heavily.

Josef did not mean this unkindly but, after all, you had to be careful these days didn't you? The Government people were always telling you to be careful. They were always telling you not to let strangers into your home and to keep an eye on your belongings and be safe and not to take chances. Yet here he was, out of kindness for the stranger in our midst, and common humanity, getting ready to open his door to this strange little man. He was just pondering the possibility of decently absolving himself from the obligations of hospitality when he happened to glance over at his new companion only to find that he was not there any more. He thought for a split second that he might have imagined the encounter and that he was, perhaps, not feeling quite as well as he had supposed but, on turning to look back down the path, he could see his little clown, some distance back, hunkered down and trying to coax yet another furry tree dweller toward the gift in the palm of his outstretched hand. After a long, tense moment the creature collected its prize and darted off. Josef clapped. Buster beamed and took a bow.

The old man was now as sure of Buster as Buster was of him. A new friend is a wonderful thing thought Josef, even at this late hour. Surely such a thing as a new friend was a gift from God.

As they walked toward Princes Street together, the old man thought with the pleasure of anticipation that only the truly compassionate know, of the various ways in which he could bestow hospitality on his new companion. He was looking forward to the sound of laughter in his silent room.

An hour later, in that very room, on the very northern edge of the New Town, Buster waited as patiently as his grumbling stomach would allow while the old man prepared a tray of cakes, biscuits and tea for them both.

The room had been Josef's living quarters for decades and now the old man did not venture out of it any more than he could help and so it was hardly surprising that the place bulged with the accumulated clutter of a long and studious life.

Buster thoroughly approved, though. He felt that he was in the presence of a very wise and learned man, for surely only learned men were allowed to leave books and papers scattered around as they pleased. Learned men had more important things to do than tidy up after them.

He made an extra effort to take his mind off his rumbling stomach by making a deeper study of the room. The curtains were of a heavy rich, silky material with a motif picked out in gold brocade which had faded badly through the years. Like the threadbare carpet, the curtains had been expensive but now, like their owner, they were seeing out their last days.

The furniture was all, with the exception of the coffee table which was newish and cheap-looking, old, dark and heavy and Buster felt a sudden stab of pity for the old man. It was a cosy room, certainly, but he suspected that his new friend spent too much time in it on his own and he doubted that many visitors came knocking at the door. People only seemed comfortable with new things these days and they did not make enough time for old men who talked slowly of old, forgotten things.

Not a moment too soon a tray was set down before him, tea was poured and Buster happily worked his way through a generous wedge of Dundee cake.

The old man took pleasure in his new friend's appetite and seemed to have read his mind as, with a sweep of his arm, he said. "See, I have friends with me all the time."

Buster looked around the room, uncomprehendingly.

"See. See," Josef persisted, jabbing a bony finger at this point and that point around the room.

Still his guest did not catch on.

"Look, look," Josef implored, more in amusement than irritation. Only then was Buster fully aware of them. On practically every surface in the room there was a framed photograph of some individual or group of people. He could not think how it was that he had missed them for so long.

The old man switched on the lamp whose glow made the room feel like a happier place altogether and the two companions sipped their tea and talked about past friendships and places they had seen and likes and dislikes and the blessed inconsequentialities of every day life until Buster, seeing that Josef was having trouble keeping his eyes open, diplomatically bade his new friend and landlord goodnight.

A MEETING

Buster liked the lemon bathroom walls. They were bright and sunny and, apart from the Tiffany lamp in Josef's room, they were, by far, the most cheerful thing that he had seen in this strange house so far.

The steam in the bathroom was so thick now that you could have cut it with a knife. The cares of the world and the weariness of his travels were far away and Buster sighed with unadulterated contentment and stroked the great white mound of his belly in slow, circular movements and in this state of bliss he was starting to nod off when he heard the door handle being tried.

"Sorry," said a nervous sounding female voice and then there was the sound of slippered feet retreating along the corridor. Buster had tried to say something but when he opened his mouth all that came out was a yawn.

The second trying of the door handle came a full fifteen minutes later and it was just loud enough to wake Buster who found that the water had turned cold. Without realising what had woken him he reached for the hot water tap.

"Oh for heaven's sake!" The voice was several notches more tightly strung this time. "How much longer are you going to be?" In a vain attempt to keep the world at bay for a little longer, and to avoid conflict, which he disliked even more than small portions, Buster turned the hot water tap on full in the hope that the sound of gushing water would drown out this rude intrusion on his reverie.

He almost scalded himself in the process but the ruse worked. Whoever it was beat another retreat, leaving Buster to complete his ablutions to his own satisfaction and, in his own sweet time, he left the bathroom and started up the stairs to his attic room. "Excuuuuuse me!!!"

If the voice was highly strung before, it was bordering on the hysterical now and the new house guest stopped dead in his tracks. He turned and peered timidly over the banister to the landing below where he could see a statuesque woman in her early forties glowering up at him. Her mouth, now taut and angry, seemed to have been superimposed on to what were otherwise rather pleasant features. Just at the moment, however, such details were lost on a petrified Buster.

"I don't know who you are," said the angry mouth, "but in this house we try to show each other a little consideration."

If she was being completely honest Miss Laird would have had to admit that there was no real basis for this claim but, then again, you had to say that sort of thing in this sort of situation, didn't you? You had to shore up your position with all the moral authority that you could muster.

"You've been in that blessed bathroom for an absolute age. There ARE other people in this house, you know. Or didn't you think of them?"

All that Miss Laird could see from her position were a pair of bulging eyes and a mouth that seemed to open and shut with the regularity of a goldfish and, probably, she thought, with about as much comprehension. Where, she wondered, did the old man find these characters?

Then, entirely without warning, she felt the anger slip away from her. She was tired after a long, difficult day and it was too much like hard work to hang on to it. She waved

Buster away with a "Don't be so thoughtless next time" and then shut the bathroom door behind her.

Buster was suitably contrite as he climbed into his bed. The mad lady had been right after all. He had just been thinking of himself – again. He always tried not to of course and, much of the time, he could be as considerate as the next person. He would have to do better, though, – starting tomorrow.

All the same, he had a strong feeling that it was not just him hogging the bathroom that had bothered the lady. Behind that angry mouth and its voice he had sensed some undefined sadness. In fact he sensed the same thing everywhere in this house. It hung in the air like a black cloud that refused to move to another part of the sky.

Buster looked at the little rosebuds on the wallpaper all around him and fancied that even they sensed the sadness too and, therefore, saw no point in making the effort to spread into bloom. He also knew that, if he let it, this cloud, or whatever it was, would seep into his bones and then he too might be swallowed up in the sadness, so he said his usual bed time prayer and felt better and knew that he could sleep now without fear.

As his eyes grew heavy, he turned, as he did every night, to that long ago and happy past and then came the old familiar faces. Familiar arms stretched out to him and the old, beloved voices sang him to sleep as they had every night for such a long time.

3

SATURDAY ...

AND THE SUN IS SHINING

Buster stood at the bus stop waiting for the No. 27 which would take him up the hill and into the centre of Edinburgh. His nose twitched as if he were a cat sniffing out the day's possibilities. Faintly, on the breeze, he could pick up the sound of the bustle of traffic coming from the City Centre and he struggled manfully to contain his excitement. Today, he had decided, would be a day of adventure and exploration.

In all his travels there was one thing that he had learnt above all others and that was that there was nothing, nothing in all the world as fine as that first morning in a new city. This was especially true on a morning like this when the sun had brushed down the tired old roofs of the New Town and softened the brick and the stone and made them new again.

He had already decided on his first port of call – the big Castle that towered above Princes Street Gardens where he had fed the squirrels only yesterday and he was just mulling over the excitements that the Castle might hold and whether or not there would be a tea room on the premises, when one of Edinburgh's maroon and white double decker buses pulled up at the stop across the road. As soon as he clapped eyes on the vehicle all thoughts of the Castle slipped from his mind for, splashed across the side of the vehicle was a huge colour reproduction of a painting advertising an exhibition of the French Impressionists in the big gallery just off Princes Street. He did not know much about Art but, like many another, he "KNEW WHAT HE LIKED" and he liked what he saw.

The painting was a picnic scene, the one set on the Bois de Boulogne that most of you will be familiar with. Buster, the simple soul, was not familiar with it at all but he was completely beguiled by the spirit of uncomplicated happiness captured within its frame. He needed to see the lady in the cornflower blue dress again and the jolly fat man with the beard. He wanted to see the sunlight dappling the picnic table and the warmth and joy of a moment that would never end.

The gallery itself was not hard to find as there was another huge reproduction of the painting on a hoarding a few yards away from the entrance, but it was spattered with mud, and some other materials of uncertain provenance and torn at one corner. The sight did not satisfy Buster in the slightest. He did not feel that it did this glimpse of Paradise justice at all. Daunting though the prospect was, he felt compelled, as metal to a magnet, to pass through the intimidating doors of the gallery and claim his "prize". At the entrance of the first of the gallery's rooms he asked the attendant where he could find "his" painting but the man, who clearly had difficulties in understanding what Buster was saying, and no great interest in finding out, waved him away in the direction of a collection of Dutch Still Lifes.

In that room Buster searched diligently along a line of paintings but, much to his mounting frustration, all he could see were studies of flowers in glass bowls or tables strewn with dead rabbits and game birds whose lifeless eyes stared up at ancient ceilings. He was incensed. This was no fun at all. It was profoundly depressing. He wanted his spirits raised, not have them sink into his boots.

When he had calmed down a bit he began to suspect that there was some trickery afoot and that the unhelpful attendant might, just might, have sent him on a wild goose chase for the purposes of his own amusement. This was not entirely paranoia on his part, for he had had plenty of experience of involuntarily providing amusement for people whose hearts were, shall we just say, less than pure.

Normally, Buster would take the line of least resistance when he suspected that he had been slighted in some way. He knew that the world was the way that it was and that the finer feelings of such as he did not really signify, but on this occasion he was not going to be trifled with. He was determined to bask in the happy reflection *Saturday ... and the Sun is Shining* of "his" painting. He was not going to be denied this innocent and necessary pleasure.

A second attendant regarded Buster with barely concealed contempt for a long moment before something clicked into place in his municipally trained mind. The man had read in his daily paper, only that very morning, about a shocking, and as yet unexplained, spate of vandalism to the nation's great paintings and the more that he saw of the specimen in front of him the more he grew certain that he had a potential Art slasher on his hands, a threat to the country's artistic heritage ... possibly even an anarchist! Surely those bulging eyes indicated some sort of imbalance or another.

SATURDAY ... AND THE SUN IS SHINING

It was all the evidence that a conscientious guardian of the nation's culture needed. Or, to be more accurate, it was all the evidence that HE needed and so, without any further warning, the man placed a large hand on Buster's back and propelled him towards the stairs leading down to the gift shop and the main door. The official's tea break was overdue so he did not even bother to escort his anarchist to the bottom of the stairs, but merely contented himself with watching the miscreant's scowling retreat. Buster did not bother turning around to throw his tormentor a dirty look. What would have been the point? It would not have brought him any closer to the picture and if he had made too much of a fuss they might have called a constable. He might have been told to "get out of town" like in the cowboy pictures or, worse, they could send him to prison. He had a terror of being locked up and being ordered around. Much better, he thought, in poetic vein, to be like the Spring breeze and held down by no man.

However, just before he was about to exit the gallery he had an idea. The gift shop sold postcards of all the Great Paintings, did they not? Surely, they would have one of the picnic scene and then he could tuck it into his pocket and gaze upon it whenever he wanted.

As he turned the postcard carousel this way and that it squeaked and groaned. It sounded to Buster like the noise old Josef made when he was excited and the amusement this gave him made him forget about his search.

Not content toying with one carousel he waddled over to its neighbour and repeated the exercise. After all, maybe IT made a different sound.

SATURDAY ... AND THE SUN IS SHINING

The gift shop's staff and customers were aware of his mischief by now. The noise grated on every ear. People tutted. People gave him dirty looks. People whispered unkind comments to one another. He didn't care. He was having fun.

The stern lady in charge of the sales counter did not agree. She told him to stop immediately or she would send for reinforcements.

That put the proverbial "tin lid" on it for Buster. He had just about had all he could take from the forces of officialdom for one day. Pointedly, he brought this second carousel (which, incidentally did sound a little different) to a grinding, teeth jarring halt. Suddenly, the silence in the Gift Shop was absolute and every eye was fixed on the shabby little hooligan as everyone wondered what he would do next.

Now that he was the centre of attention he decided to make the most of the situation. He stepped forward a pace or two, raised two fingers to the lady behind the counter, bowed low to the customers, who, after all, had not been the ones responsible for thwarting him, and scuttled out of this humourless establishment before retribution had a chance to catch up with him.

4

DRISCOLL RISES

Driscoll turned in his half sleep to face the rays of the confident April sun that was now probing every corner of his room through a gap in the curtains, and uttered one of the stronger Anglo Saxon oaths. As far as he was concerned the sun was an unwelcome visitor. The sun was for the living, after all, and, as hung over as he was, he was not sure that he possessed the minimum qualifications for that state.

He hankered after a painless oblivion but, still, the sun persisted. It had a duty to illuminate everything in its path and the ageing Embezzler, languishing in his "scratcher", was not going to be an exception.

Eventually, Driscoll forced open one red and watery eye, blinked and repeated the oath, but more vehemently this time. He wondered, wearily, why day had to follow day quite so relentlessly. If only the world would stop careering around for a wee while, a body might have a chance to catch his breath long enough to stop and work things out, instead of having Time dragging him along by the scruff of his neck.

Finally, giving up on oblivion in the meantime, he swung his skinny, varicose-veined, legs over the edge of the bed and sat, for a while, with his elbows on his knees and his head in his hands. He was not for opening the curtains just yet. There was some comfort and safety in this half-lit world and he wanted to hang on to it for a little longer. If he could not hold back time at least he could keep the full power of that celestial bully out of his own little world for just a little while more.

He lit a cigarette and waited for the customary coughing fit to subside before, once again, surrendering to the facts. He could not turn back time and undo what he had done, and the money – "that money" – was running out fast. He reckoned that, at best, he had enough for another month and then what? He took a long deep drag on his Capstan Full Strength and watched the dovetailing spirals of blue smoke make their unconcerned way up to the ceiling.

He allowed himself a mirthless smile. After all, these twisted spirals of smoke were a perfect metaphor for his own convoluted affairs.

Once upon a time this situation would not have bothered him so much. He would have done the necessary ducking and diving. He might even have been sharp enough and quick enough to turn the situation around and so avoid retribution. Even if the worst had come to the worst and he had ended up doing time he would have been all right. When he was young he had had the necessary energy. When he was young he had had resilience. When he was young he had not allowed himself to care about very much at all. Now, though, sitting on the edge of his mouldy bed, sullied by who knew how many unknown bodies, he felt the last pretence of youth and vigour draining out of him. He fancied that he could actually feel the blood congeal in his veins. He was tired, bone tired. What he really wanted to do was hand himself in and so put a stop to the torment of the next few weeks. He wanted to stop the army of sullen, gloomy and fear filled hours in their tracks – but he was afraid. Like a reluctant parachutist he needed some-one, or something, to give him a mighty push out into the unknown.

He stubbed out the Capstan and struggled over to the curtains and pulled them open. The full power of the sun blinded him and he staggered back towards his bed where he noticed a copy of The Racing Post lying on the floor at the foot of it.

He picked it up and turned to that day's races. He had not actually been intending to bet today but, then again, these days he clung gratefully to any thing that could divert his attention from thoughts of his imminent future.

Suddenly, a burst of light exploded in his head. There it was! There it was! Kelso Races. 3.40. Sun King. 100-1.

Driscoll had been surprised to find that working on the elaborate plans for his own martyrdom had left him with such a ferocious appetite. Somewhere, at the back of his mind, there had been a vague notion that, by this point, he should be still, calm and resigned to his fate. His notion had not stretched to sausage, bacon, black pudding, two fried eggs, beans and toast and tea at the "Chat and Choo" but here he was with his "stomach about to cut his throat."

The waitress brought his "Belly Buster Breakfast Special" over and he seasoned his meal with large dollops of tomato ketchup and self congratulation. The whole plan had been worked out with military precision and he was set to go out in a blaze of glory at precisely 3.40 p.m. that afternoon.

He dipped a morsel of sausage into his egg yolk and worked it vigorously around. He grinned in triumph as a rivulet of yellow ran over a rasher of bacon. He was now back in control. A "do-er", not just some one who is "done to".

Sun King. 100-1. A gift. One brief race and, provided he held his nerve, he could lay down his burden forever. Sun King, eh? He laughed so hard he almost choked on his black pudding. No chance that monkey was going to come up with the goods.

He would have to put every penny on it though. That meant EVERY single penny that he had in the world. That way he would have nowhere else to go and no means of running away. He would HAVE to give himself up and get it all over with. All decisions after that glorious moment would be made for him – just as they were in his army days.

He sniggered into his tea cup. What a release. What a relief. Ironically, he thought I *will* be released, for am I not in a "prison" now – one of my own making?

Ah, the sweet relief of it all. No more jangling nerves as he saw his reserves of cash dwindle day by day. No more haunted nights, twisting and turning in that rancid pit as he wondered how long he could keep body and soul together. No more fear about being nabbed if he broke cover and tried to get a real job and definitely no need to go cap in hand to the Tindall Brothers for a loan that he would never be able to afford to repay anyway. There was a thought to keep you awake at night – the Law and the Tindall Brothers on your erse at the same time!

No, Driscoll boy, he thought, no more of that. You'll be the Captain of your own ship again. The master of your soul.

5
FEEDING THE INNER MAN

Buster was in a sour mood for a long time after his disappointment in the Gallery and he strode along, shoulders hunched, muttering to himself, which only served to make people point and stare which, in turn, only served, in that cyclical way of things to make his mood even more sour.

After a while, he sat down on a bench in Princes Street and forced himself to calm down in the manner which he had been taught. He breathed deeply and slowly as he watched the world passing by but, just as he was making his way back to his customary sunny disposition, the "one o' clock gun" was fired from the Castle Esplanade. Buster jumped from the bench, his heart thumped in his chest and he wondered if the City was under attack from some invading army. It was all very disconcerting.

When the old lady who had been sitting at the other end of the bench saw his reaction, she took the time to explain about the gun. Reassured, Buster's face lit up like Christmas Tree lights. If it was one o clock it was half way through lunch time.

He sprang to his feet, bowed low and thanked the lady profusely for bringing him such good news. Now all he needed to do was find an establishment worthy of his appetite.

Finlay's was a bustling, cheerful place with a large ground floor and a flight of stairs that led up to a balcony where happy diners beamed down at the rest of the world.

A thought occurred to Buster. Perhaps the portions were bigger up there but, then again, you might have to pay more for the view, but, then again, bigger portions were bigger portions. You just never knew how these things were decided and it was better not to risk losing out. Whatever was the case, he thought that it would be a delightful novelty to have such a spectacular view as he tucked into his chicken and chips.

He had only taken a few steps towards the stairs when the fountain on the other side of the ground floor caught his eye. He was transfixed. He had never seen a fountain in a restaurant before and he approached the glinting, sparkling water with some reverence and, seeing a spattering of coins lying on the tiles beneath the water, realised, with delight, that it would be appropriate to make a wish.

Suddenly, he was friends with the city again. Earlier insults and slights were forgotten as he fished in his pockets and pulled out three coins and threw one in as he made each wish.

He had intended to donate all three wishes for the good of others but gluttony got the better of him and so his last wish was that his eagerly awaited lunch would be every bit as appetising and generously proportioned as it looked on the picture in the window. Unbeknown to him, however, while his attention had been taken up with the fountain, a nervous lady customer, certain that Buster was representative of one of the more dangerous forms of lunacy, had alerted the management.

The first he knew of this development was the urgent prodding of his shoulder. Buster, who had not long completed his last wish, was most impressed. Seldom had any of his wishes ever been granted so expeditiously.

He asked the manageress, owner of the aforesaid finger, if the chicken dish was exactly as depicted in the advert – not of course, that he was accusing Finlay's of any skulduggery – and just to be sure he gave the bewildered woman a detailed description of exactly how he thought such a dish should be set before a discerning diner such as himself.

The woman stood open-mouthed for a long moment. She wagged a finger – yes that one – at Buster and was about to read him the Riot Act but then thought better of it and made a B line for the kitchen. A moment later she returned, flanked by a pair of burly employees in kitchen whites.

Buster, obliging as ever, was more than willing to repeat his instructions if it helped the restaurant folk to do their job properly but, as things turned out, there was to be no time for conversation. His feet barely touched Finlay's plush carpet as he was escorted off the premises and now he was out on the street again … sans chicken … sans chips.

Later he found solace by way of the "Special Fish Tea" at Esposito's Tea Room, whose portions were as large as their premises were small.

FEEDING THE INNER MAN

It wasn't quite the same though. He would really rather have had that juicy chicken and the fat chips in the picture in Finlay's window and he knew that he would feel that way until the picture had faded from his mind.

6

THE HOUR OF GLORY APPROACHES

In the Guild Bar, midway through Saturday afternoon, Driscoll looked at his watch, drained his glass and rose from his stool – but then had second thoughts. He could just about fit one more in and there was no point in hanging about the bookies any longer than absolutely necessary. It was a depressing place even when you *were* riding high, metaphorically speaking, on some nag or another.

Aye, definitely time for another. Not that he needed Dutch Courage, though. Oh no, he was a man who had decided to take life by the scruff of the neck and dare it to do its worst.

"Same again, chief?"

Billy set down a double on the counter and said, in as disinterested a manner as he could manage to fake."What's the story wi' you and the good stuff today?"

Driscoll, never slow to sniff out an insult, resented the implication that the "good stuff" was, somehow, a bit TOO good for him, and was about to tell the impudent sod to go and ^%***^ himself but, instead, he saw an opportunity to set his own personal legend rolling and so he told Billy about the bet, but not the reason for it, still less the part that the Law would later play in the proceedings.

The impudent bar steward studied the expression on Driscoll's face more closely than he would the lines on his payslip and, after a long moment's reflection, came to his considered conclusion. "Yer aff yer heid!"

Driscoll radiated serenity.

"On the contrary, son, it's the one sane thing I've done these past few years."

Billy, the ever loquacious, was, for once, lost for words – but, unfortunately, not for long.

"You got religion or something?"

Driscoll, by now positively immersed in a warm bath of serenity, merely smiled an enigmatic smile. He was saying nothing. He was enjoying this cocksure wee bastard's discomfiture too much.

Billy persisted though. It was what Billy did. "Your whole wedge on a 100-1 no hoper?"

Driscoll would not be drawn into any more detail. He had said enough for his purpose. His Mona Lisa smile was in danger of breaking out beyond the confines of his face.

"Well, dinnae expect any credit in here then, that's all I'm sayin'" said Billy, who had an exaggerated sense of his place in the Guild's staff hierarchy, before walking the length of the bar to serve another customer.

Driscoll sat nursing his Lagavuillin and burning to tell the little swine why he would shortly be freed from all financial fetters and would, therefore, have no need to throw himself on anybody's mercy but, if the legend was going to have a chance to grow, he was going to have to keep his piehole firmly zipped. The wee "yak" had served his purpose though. Even now his flapping tongue was spreading the "legend" to every nook and cranny of the Guild Bar.

On every tongue there was a variation of the same question: "Who was this in their midst, hero or madman?"

3.40 galloped on. They would not have long to wait for an answer.

7
THE RACE IS RUN

In a few minutes Driscoll was standing at the entrance to the bookies, next door to the Guild, fishing in the pocket of his regimental blazer for the sacrificial wad of cash, when a wave of humanity propelled him through the door.

This was not how he had planned it. Where was the dignity here, for pity's sake? He took a moment to collect himself and throw a dirty look over his shoulder before striding manfully up to the cashier's desk, employing what he liked to think of as his full military bearing as he did so. Meanwhile his newly gathered throng of admirers stuck like a rash to his back.

"Sun King. 3.40. Kelso," said Driscoll in clipped military manner, laying the money in the cashier's tray. Just to underline his nonchalance he ran his hand languidly through his wavy grey and nicotine stained hair.

Marie counted the money before asking with an incredulous squeak, "What, all of it?"

"Every last penny, sweetheart," said the hero of the hour.

He thought there might have been a burst of hip hoorays or, at the very least, a manly clap on the back but, instead there was just a deafening silence.

Every man in the room looked as if he had just been punched very hard in the solar plexus by a mailed fist as the implications of Driscoll's deed struck home for the first time. Every man in the room had just put the rent money, his wife's wedding ring and the children's future on the back of a 100-1 no-hope monkey.

Driscoll was the only one within those four walls who was completely unconcerned as the race started.

At first, things went exactly according to his master plan. The only possible explanation for Sun King's performance was that no-one had explained to the animal the importance of the occasion. It seemed for all the world as if it was out for a leisurely walk in the Spring sunshine – possibly on doctor's orders – and the bookies was appropriately full of contorted faces frozen in masks of horror. All hearts were pounding in unison. Each man felt that, at that very moment, money was being siphoned out of his own pocket and that he would soon be trudging a weary path home to tell an irate wife why the rent or mortgage would not be paid that month and why the family diet might be a little monotonous for a while.

Driscoll, however, had escaped to a higher plane. He was not exactly smiling but his features had fallen into a sort of sweet repose. The proverbial great weight had fallen from his shoulders and his rheumy eyes moistened with tears of relief. His way was clear now. No need to hide. No need to walk around looking over his shoulder any more. To-night he would sleep soundly in a police cell. His sins would be some one else's problems for he would have achieved absolution.

Sure that the race was now a foregone conclusion, he turned to leave the bookies and start out on his road to martyrdom but, before he could even lay a hand on the door knob, the radio crackled with the sound of the commentator's hysterical voice. "Incredible. Just incredible!" it screamed. "I've never seen anything like this in all my years at the races!"

Driscoll froze, stricken.

Sun King seemed, albeit belatedly, to have finally understood what the words "horse race" actually meant and was proving most eager to make up for lost time. In fact, right at that moment, the animal was "eating up the opposition in a demented dash for the finishing line".

The radio man quipped that perhaps Sun King had just remembered an urgent appointment Then, on a more serious note, he criticised the jockey for the amount of whip he was using.

The other punters greeted the comment with gales of nervous laughter but Driscoll wasn't laughing and, before he could stop himself, he bawled out …

"Aye, leave the poor beast alone. You'll lay its ribs bare." No sooner had he said it, though, than the race was over. The deed was done and he was stuck with it.

Yes, the race was run and won and Sun King was heading for a "royal reception" in the paddock as the bookies office erupted in a roar that could have been heard in Kelso itself.

Driscoll slumped against the wall, staring ahead, hollow-eyed, like a soldier with the "2,000-yard stare".

When the cacophony subsided all eyes turned to the man of the moment who by this time had managed to pull himself together and was now standing fully erect and rooted to the spot.

After an awkward few moments silence, little Eck Munro, who lived above the Pie Shop around the corner, and who had not had a win since last "Pancake Tuesday", stepped forward, took a gentle hold of his new hero's arm and led him through the crowd which silently and respectfully parted to let Driscoll make his way triumphantly to the cashier's window.

Thomas Tyrone Driscoll had just been canonised the patron saint of hopeful losers by this gathering and, as such, was led in a reverent procession back to the Guild Bar where he set the seal on the proceedings by buying each of his new "congregation" a drink. He was their man now. He was the man that had proved that, just sometimes, two and two can make five. Yes, he was their man all right and that wouldn't change now even if they had caught him kicking a day-old kitten the length and breadth of the Guild Bar.

In every corner his legend was being embellished by his grateful followers who had been given a brief holiday from that universal truth that: "YOU CAN'T GET SOMETHING FOR NOTHING!!!!!!!"

Everyone in the bar was relaxed and unconcerned with the twists and turns of fate – everyone except Driscoll. In a few short moments one of those aforementioned twists had placed the burden squarely back on his arthritic shoulders and he sat staring at his own morose reflection in a brass beer font. His anguished features were, in turn, a perfect reflection of the turmoil that now raged within him.

He wept silent tears for his lost absolution and the thing that twisted most in his gut was the fact that he really HAD intended to hand himself in but who would believe him now. Part of him was beginning to doubt it himself. Fate had prevented him from making one of the few worthwhile gestures of his entire miserable life.

He had wanted, with an earnestness that he no longer thought himself capable of, to lay down his burden and find himself a new skin that would fit him better than the one that he had been forced to inhabit for so long.

He wanted to sleep now. That was all. He wanted to go home and sink into that tainted bed and sleep. If he could not have absolution he would settle for some small measure of oblivion.

8

THE EVENING'S VELVET EMBRACE

The day had, so far, ticked along quite nicely for Miss Elizabeth Laird in the small, but exclusive, hat shop that she managed in the City's West End. No alarms or excursions. No returns and no awkward customers. And … she had managed to sell that orange monstrosity that Lachlan, her boss, had insisted she place slap bang in the middle of the window as if it was, somehow, the Rolls Royce of all hats.

Lachlan, she thought, was an intelligent man, but he did not know hats and she fervently hoped that he was better at picking restaurants and she simpered at the thought of the evening that stretched out ahead of her, sweet and velvety with promise.

And the last of the business day continued to tick uneventfully away, seasoned by the odd moment of pleasurable conjecture about what the hours ahead might hold.

In due course, Miss Laird bade her assistant good night, locked up the shop and set off along William Street toward her evening of adventure.

The invitation had come as a complete surprise to her and had been delivered in such a casual manner that she had been sure that her ears had deceived her. At first, she had doubted that it was a bona fide "date" but then, she reasoned, surely no-body invites a girl out to dinner on a Saturday night unless it is a "date". Surely? No, of course not, and that speck of doubt was stamped further into the dust with her every step.

She exuded confidence now. She was fully prepared to join the ranks of the loved this evening. She knew that Lachlan was fond of her and, for her part, she had been ready to make that jump from friend to lover. She had seen it happen to others. Why shouldn't it be her turn now?

What was so strange about Elizabeth Laird finding her place among the needed of this world and why should she not be rescued from the constant rattle of her own thoughts?

Her sense of compassion, though, even amid the jangle of her own excitement, was for those for whom this April evening would be just another evening but, at the same time, she already considered herself apart from them. She no longer numbered herself among the grey, anonymous crowd who you didn't even notice when you were in the middle of their throng for, had she not just joined the ranks of those who were loved and, so, was she not now truly alive?

It was the old, pre-epiphany, Driscoll who woke again just after six that evening. His blistered heart had just found room for yet another grudge. Now it railed against fate itself. Well, who among us could blame him for that?

How many of us, in times of inner turmoil, have "knelt" before Fate and offered this sacrifice or that in return for things going our way for a little while, only to have the gesture flung back in our face in this way or that? It's too much isn't it? You feel such a fool don't you?

THE EVENING'S VELVET EMBRACE

Driscoll stood by the window, sucking on a Capstan Full Strength and watching the retreating sun follow its preordained path.

"Sun King," he snorted. "The Bastard."

Well, he thought, if that was the way it was going to be, he would go his own way and Fate could go and **********%@ itself. After all, if Fate had thwarted him you could also argue that he had managed to poke fate in the eye. He had money now, had he not? How did Fate know that he had not been playing a game of double bluff? How did Fate know that he had not "slipped one past it"? No, all in all, he reckoned that this time Fate had shot itself squarely in the foot.

Driscoll ran his discoloured tongue around his parched lips. The way he saw it, he was bankrolled for the rest of this year anyway and the good times would start just as soon as he could get his hands on a glass of whisky.

In a room along the hall, Elizabeth Laird, spinster, 42, showed a good deal more grace as she waited for the evening and her new life to properly begin. She had just had a bowl of soup and was sipping a dry sherry to steady her nerves.

It seemed to work. The Chinese Acrobat in her stomach had stopped turning somersaults and she was now relaxed and confident that she would hear the main doorbell from her room and that, in just a few moments, she could be downstairs opening it before some helpful soul could let Lachlan in to see the depths to which she had sunk.

THE EVENING'S VELVET EMBRACE

That was only fair. This house was not really part of her anyway, so why should it be allowed to cling to her like some malignant shadow? Its dilapidation and general air of melancholy and failed lives could only muddy the waters between Lachlan and herself.

Still, now that she stood firmly on the path that would lead her away from this room, she could allow herself a certain aesthetic pleasure in the beauty that the fading sun had brought to its slow leaving of it.

That same sun, so detested by Driscoll, here ennobled burnished wood, faded fabric and even her own reflection in the mirror on the door of her wardrobe. All pleasingly melancholic she thought, but only if you had a brighter world to escape to, which of course she did.

So there sat Miss Elizabeth Laird, spinster 42, manageress of the most respected hat shop in the whole of Edinburgh ... a child dressed in her best frock and waiting to be invited to the party.

At exactly 6.59 p.m. ...

... Driscoll was secreting his ill-gotten gains under a pile of soiled clothing at the bottom of the wardrobe in his room.

... Josef Straczynski was listening to an elderly, scratched recording of Clair De Lune and drifting in and out of sleep between the present and his other, lost world.

... Miss Laird sat patiently in her room, her hands clasped, as if in prayer.

THE EVENING'S VELVET EMBRACE

THE EVENING'S VELVET EMBRACE

At exactly 6.59 the phone in the hall rang.

At this point I feel I must step into the fray to protect this decent lady's finer feelings for, as you have probably guessed, the phone call was not bringing the news Miss Laird wanted to hear.

The "date" was, after all, just a business meeting. Lachlan, knowing that her social life was almost non existent – though she had gone to great lengths to hide this fact – thought he would treat his valued employee to a nice dinner while he slipped in a few promotional ideas that he wished her to implement over the next few months.

In Lachlan's tidy mind this would save time later and also give her an evening away from the radio and Saturday Night Theatre. He was a decent sort but not especially perceptive. He had no idea that she was smitten with him, mainly because he was a modest sort of a man and that was one of the chief reasons that she WAS so smitten with him.

I will cut a long story short. An ex-Army chum of Lachlan's had phoned to say that he was in town for the week-end and Lachlan, being loyal to his friends – another trait that Elizabeth valued greatly – decided that to-night, that was where his loyalties lay.

He apologised profusely, of course, and assured Elizabeth that it was only a postponement and that they would have another chance to "cook the books over some chow soon".

She had managed to keep any suggestion of a quaver out of her voice while she was still holding the phone but her resolve not to let the "whole bloody fiasco" get her down lasted only as long as it took her to get back to her room and close the door on the rest of the world.

Once safely back in her own little world, she settled herself in front of a bottle of Copper Beech Sherry and drained it in the course of the next ninety minutes, while marvelling at her ability to cry so much without succumbing to dehydration.

9
THE GHOST OF A SMILE

The Gladstone could not exactly be described as the best feature of the elegant Georgian Square in which it stood. Its heyday, as a smart Edinburgh Hotel, had been over for a good couple of decades now but there were still some echoes of its pre-war glory. Once it had been the haunt of Edinburgh's "legal eagles", senior civil servants and even the "India men" who had returned to the old country after a lifetime of service on the subcontinent but, nowadays, you were more likely to find double glazing salesmen or shifty town councillors propping up the bar.

Driscoll, however, had a sneaking admiration for the place although it was not an establishment that he had frequented very often, except for the odd occasion when he was in the vicinity and an excess of alcohol had helped him to overcome his deep seated inferiority complex. Funny, isn't it, how bombastic, lifelong bullies will let themselves be intimidated by simple things like a hotel entrance?

To-night was different though. To-night he was every man's equal for had he not just put one over on Fate itself? The alcohol imbibed in various bars in Stockbridge had imbued Driscoll with a surface veneer that was very effective in shielding him from the realities of everyday life. Even the mirror in the Men's Room kept the truth from him. Circumstance had arranged a temporary, charmed existence for him.

He splashed his face in the sink and the face that he saw looking back at him no longer had the mottled complexion of the confirmed toper. Thirty years, at least, had been stripped away by this alcoholic mirage and now he felt a young man's optimism as far as the night ahead was concerned. It was Saturday night, after all, and nothing like the mean and desperate Saturday nights of his recent past, either.

As he slicked his hair back he remembered his glory days when Saturday nights were simply a matter of donning your best bib and tucker and a confident smile. After a few drinks anything was possible and he had already had much more than just a few drinks. His ablutions complete, he settled himself on a stool at the end of the bar and proceeded to do what he had always wanted to, but only now could afford, which was to work his way through the Gladstone's fine collection of malts which stretched the length of the bar's gantry.

After the Balvenie, he bought he himself a cigar. It was an appropriate night for a cigar he thought. It was certainly an expensive cigar but Driscoll, who did not know much about such things, also did not know that this particular item was some way past its best.

Still, he took an exaggerated pleasure in rolling the large object between his fingers and watching the beefy smoke rings as they rose high above him. Then he moved onto the Glen Morangie and, after that, the Lagavuillin.

Driscoll was pacing himself though. He may not have accrued much knowledge in his journey through this "Vale of Tears" but he knew and respected the Malts and would never insult them by guzzling.

He also knew that, given the amount of booze that he had already consumed, he stood no chance whatsoever of getting even half way to the end of the Gantry, but that was not the point. The point was that, owing to Sun King, he was free to embark upon the adventure. The point was also that his new riches, wrested this day from Fate's thorny paw would keep him from the aggravations of the world for the foreseeable future and, then again, the real bloody point was that he had found a "cosy corner" here in the dear old Gladstone – safe from icy reality – and he would cling to it for just as long as he could.

"I like to see a man enjoy a good cigar."

Driscoll turned from his reverie to see a woman, probably in her mid thirties, and blonde, but not in a particularly provocative way. Her hair was shortish and straight and it framed the delicate features of a face which, if it hadn't carried a hint of weariness, would generally be considered pretty. She held out a slim hand. "Lesley," she said simply.

Driscoll stopped rolling the cigar. He was confused. Even in his inebriated state he knew that women like Lesley didn't talk to men like him. Men of his age were invisible to women under forty. It was some sort of unwritten law of the universe.

Nevertheless, he looked her up and down while at the same time trying hard not to let her see him looking her up and down. Besides, he thought slyly, were not all the usual rules set aside for tonight?

Tonight was a universe complete unto itself. The normal mean limitations of the day to day life of an ageing embezzler could not lay so much as a bony finger on this blessed night. Perhaps his new found affluence had brought some sheen of suavity to him that could only be picked up by the female of the species. This last thought chased another five years from off his shoulders.

If the haze of alcohol was kind to him, it was also kind to her. It hid her weariness from him. It hid the fact that her sleeveless, but demure, cocktail dress was frayed around the hem and that there was a small run on one of her stockings just behind the knee.

Driscoll had already decided that she was a wee "bobby dazzler", a wee honey, a classy dame and so forth, but he was still a little mystified by her sudden interest in him. It had been a very long time since any woman had even acknowledged his presence in the world and there was something about Lesley that was at once distant and yet tantalisingly familiar. He nodded in the direction of her glass which was still half full.

"Will you take a drink lass?"

She was easy to talk to and because of this Driscoll's puzzlement at her interest in him soon faded. From the little that she said on the subject of herself, he gathered that she was a business lady of some sorts, up in Edinburgh to close some deal or other.

Driscoll didn't care about the details. She was pretty, she had a pulse and she was talking to him in a way that made him feel that he had not quite fallen off the edge of the world just yet and she sat patiently through his tales of Army life, his struggles to build up a good going business, loss of the same (though he was light on the details here) and his noble struggle to rise, Phoenix like, from the ashes.

With every twist and turn of this self-serving saga, which Driscoll nimbly edited as he went along, her face carried the appropriate expression, whether it be sympathy or admiration etc., and when it came to a point where his monologue reached a particularly dramatic high, she laid her elegant, slight hand on his and stroked it sympathetically.

Driscoll felt his throat tighten and experienced a very definite prickling behind the eyes. After all, here was a man, who, for the best part of a decade had been barely visible to the world. Here was a man who was of no interest to the world, even if it could see him. Here was a man who eked out his days as a shadow in a dusty bedsit or a dingy bar lounge and now someone had shone a light into the darkness and her slim hand was, even now, coaxing him back into the land of the living.

He studied Lesley with new eyes but not yet with lust. He was drunk but he wasn't daft. He knew that that particular train had left the station a long, long time ago. Sex, as far as Driscoll was concerned, occupied the same amount of space in his head as Greek Mythology. No, he was merely assigning her a place in his own personal small gallery of saints for what she had already bestowed upon him tonight.

When he snapped to again Lesley was rummaging in her handbag. "What's the matter sweetheart?" He now felt bold enough to use the word.

"My purse. I was going to buy you a drink."

"Don't worry, doll," said Driscoll, the veritable knight errant. "I'll get it."

"No, but my purse ... and my keys." It was the hint of a wail in her voice which unnerved him.

She looked like a child about to cry and Driscoll noticed her weariness fully for the first time and suddenly he thought he recognised her from somewhere. He felt as if some squirrel was scampering through the attic of his memory, kicking up dust but without finding what it was looking for. He was suddenly overcome by a wave of compassion for this shop-worn angel.

10

A BRIEF BUT TENDER HAUNTING

As he made his way back to his lodgings, the events of the day buzzed around Buster's head like a particularly industrious swarm of bees.

There was the altercation with uniformed authority in that forbidding and mighty Hall of Culture and then there was that unpleasantness at lunchtime when all he had wanted was a good feed.

There was the young man sitting on the bench in Princes Street who had begged his love not to leave him, who had laid his heart bare for her and told her that his world would have no meaning if she was no longer in it. She had listened in silence as though she had already left and shut the door quietly behind her and Buster had tried all day to get the sound of pain in the young man's voice out of his head and only now was it fading.

There was the little girl clutching her dolly and sitting alone on the grass in Princes Street Gardens while her peers played a few yards away, ignoring her completely.

Buster had been on the point of going over and giving them a good talking to. Why did she have to be left out of all the fun? Then he thought of going over to the child and offering her one of his boiled sweets – perhaps one of the bright yellow ones to cheer her up – but his Guardian Angel had tapped him on the shoulder just in time and he remembered that his betters did not appreciate that sort of thing and, in his case at least, were very likely to misunderstand his motives. The world was always looking for monsters and bogey men and he was not going to give anyone the satisfaction of casting him as one. The little man had reluctantly left the little girl alone with her doll and walked away biting his lip and wondering why the world always seemed to choose to be cruellest to those who had done it the least harm.

Archie, beloved companion of Miss Agnes Reid, 64 St. Stephen Street, sat in the doorway of the florists staring up at the Man in the Moon in adoration. The celestial gentleman was too far away for stroking and cuddling purposes but his presence was still comforting.

Archie certainly needed comforting tonight. He could still feel the impression of the fishmonger's boot on his backside and *that* particular act of violence had been visited on him a good many hours ago now.

Also he had been nearly run over by a child on its trike and, just to round off a pig of a day, he was shut out of his very satisfactory billet because old Agnes had fallen asleep in front of the T.V. and so couldn't see or hear him as he pawed at her ground floor window and yowled his head off.

He had just accepted that he was all alone in the world when he became aware of another presence in the street.

Buster liked St. Stephen Street and was glad that it was on his way home. If the truth were told he would even have taken a detour, if necessary, for the pleasure of walking along it once again. He liked the fact that, along with the fishmonger, florists and newsagent and all the other sensible shops, there were also establishments that sold brass candle sticks and accordians and boxes of photographs of worlds vanished long ago and dusty old books which, he suspected, contained lots of useful stuff that the big, wide, whirling world had forgotten that it needed to know.

Tonight, as usual, he was not disappointed for, halfway along the street he saw something glinting in an Antique Shop and went to investigate. An oval table mirror with a heavy silver frame entwined with long, tangled flowers, picked out in relief, sat in pride of place in the middle of the window.

Buster liked mirrors and he leaned forward grinning and eager to run through his usual repertoire of funny faces before experimenting with some new ones.

His great moon face grinned back at him. What a handsome fellow he was, he thought with pleasure. He was proud of his rubber features and their ability to provide amusement. He just wished that there was someone else to enjoy this show with. Just then Archie made his presence felt by coiling in and out between Buster's legs and purring loudly.

Buster's wish had just been answered. He bent down, beaming. Archie's purring grew louder as he luxuriated in this stranger's attention and as he studied the fat moon face the animal's heart skipped a beat. Had the Man in the Moon taken pity on his miserable and humble admirer and come down to offer his subject what comfort he could?

Archie's hero held him to his heart and kissed his forehead, cuddled him and crooned into his twitching ear and waltzed around the cold night street with him.

His feline follower was ecstatic. So the moon – the beautiful, distant and silvery moon – had deigned to come down and dance with him and comfort him in his hour of despair. One thing was certain. Archie would never – pardon the pun – see the moon in the same light again.

The warmth of Buster's embrace and the soporific effect of his crooning had anaesthetized this faithful animal to the day's sorrows and he had forgotten his throbbing back side, but all good things end too quickly. Buster, suddenly remembering that he had a warm bed waiting for him and feeling that his own eventful day was now catching up with him, kissed Archie on the forehead, placed him gently down on the cold pavement and bade him a fond farewell.

Archie watched intently until Buster turned the corner at the end of the street and then he wandered back to the florist's doorway and, seeing that the Man in the Moon had arrived safely home, gave thanks for his few moments of solace.

Lesley was much more than merely upset. She was at the end of her tether. She was defeated. She sat on her stool, head drooping, as silent tears ran down her face. Out of a mixture of compassion and embarrassment Driscoll bought her a large brandy and ushered her over to a cubicle in the far corner of the bar where he listened as patiently as any priest to her story.

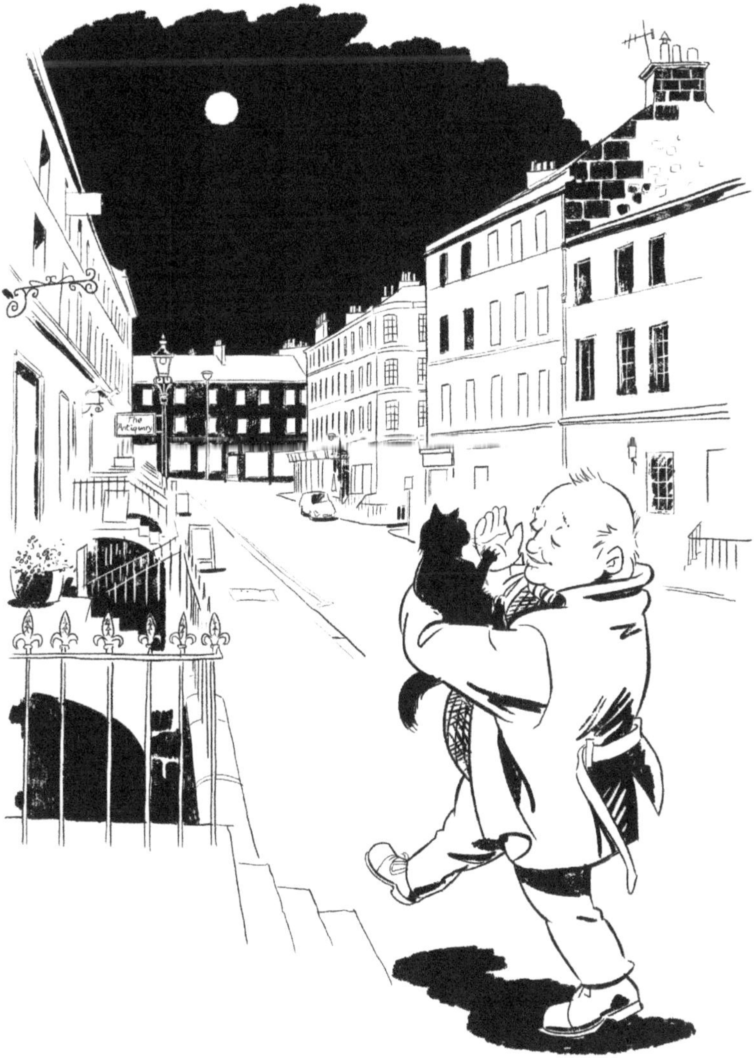
The Antiquary

It was his turn to pat her hand now. She did not flinch from the contact. She didn't acknowledge his touch but she did not flinch. She just stared silently into the middle distance as Driscoll persevered with clumsy attempts to comfort her.

She looked so vulnerable, he thought. She looked at once older and younger than her years. She looked like … he took a large mouthful of whisky in a vain attempt to wash away the thought but the squirrel lodging in the attic of his memory kept scratching.

… And she would have been about that age when he had walked out on her … and she would have been … vulnerable! There was no whisky left now and he let out an audible sigh of pain.

Lesley looked up suddenly at the sound. She slid along the seat and laid her head on his shoulder. Driscoll, unused to this level of physical intimacy these many years, looked wildly around him as if for guidance as to what to do next and imagined that every eye that met his seemed to be daring him to brush her away.

Instead, he put his arm around her and drew her closer into him. He had not been this close to another's vulnerability for a long time. He had not been this close to anyone for a long time. It occurred to him that this might just be the moment to make some small atonement for that long ago act of treachery.

In the chip shop she leant on the counter as she studied the items on the wall menu. Her face looked pinched and drawn under Vito's unforgiving strip lighting and Driscoll felt that the Fate that he had tempted a few short hours ago was retaliating with a challenge.

"Well, Thomas, are you going to repeat that old wickedness? Are you going to abandon her again?"

They sat on a street bench outside one of the New Town's Private Gardens. Lesley looked at the handsome Georgian houses on the other side of the road, obviously impressed. She smiled. "How the other half live!"

Driscoll, dreamy with alcohol and fatigue, thought that, with a smile on her face, she looked the very spit of Margaret a quarter of a century ago. If he had been sober he would have thought he was being haunted. Now he just felt as though the squirrel had moved from the attic into the pit of his stomach.

"Do you live round here Tommy?"

"Not far, but it's just a wee place. Don't let your scran get cold." She opened up the brown paper parcel licking her lips theatrically. Driscoll enjoyed the moment. After all, what can be more satisfying than feeding the hungry?

She wolfed down her food in a way that made him wonder how long it had been since her last decent meal. He was certain now that she had nowhere to rest her head for the night.

After finishing her meal, Lesley sat back with a contented sigh. She looked at him as he contemplated the enigma beside him. "You're awfully serious tonight Tommy."

He felt a strange comfort at her use of the word "tonight". It implied that they had known many nights together and that somehow she was so familiar with him that she knew what was going on in his head. It was something that used to irk him all those years ago but, right now, it was like a warm hearth on a cold night. She had breached the awful solitariness of his thoughts. "Aye, well, too cold to sit here all night."

Obediently, silently, she got up, straightened her skirt and, meekly putting her arm in his, they walked downhill through the moonlit New Town.

She chattered away about nothing in particular as they went and as she did so one small compartment after another in the embezzler's heart came back to life, rejoicing at the retreat of that perpetual silence which had been his world for so long.

11
ALL THE WARMTH OF THE PAST VISITS THE UNWORTHY DRISCOLL

When Driscoll switched the light on in his room and the bulb blew he felt strangely relieved. He did not want the evidence of his decay to be seen by anyone and particularly not this will o' the wisp creature who might fly away, like some exotic butterfly, at the slightest upset.

He had intended to make a cup of tea for them both, but the woman, who now looked like some wraith as she stood bathed in the glow of the full moon streaming in through the window, had started taking off her clothes, folding them neatly and laying them over the back of a chair at the foot of his bed.

Driscoll watched this scene with a depth of compassion that he no longer thought that his shrunken heart was capable of. He was not thinking about the possibility of sex because, even now, he did not think that there was any possibility.

He noticed, now, the clues to a pinched life evident in her clothing: the frayed hem of her dress, the ladder on one stocking, which seemed to have got much bigger since he had first seen it, the button about to fall off the little matching jacket, and now he also noticed a hole in the sole of one shoe.

Finally, she stepped out of a pair of ivory coloured "drawers" with a detached and silent grace before slipping between the covers with a grateful sigh and laying her head gently down on the pillow. Then she remembered Driscoll who was still standing with the pot of tea in his hand.

"Aren't you getting in then?"

She had a nice voice. It was clear and well modulated but he could not think of which part of England it belonged to.

"Come on you can't stand there all night holding that." He nodded towards an easy chair. "I'll kip down in that."

She studied him for a long moment, touched and amused by his awkwardness.

"Come on. Get in," she said in a mock school mistress tone.

He was too tired to argue and, besides, it had been a long time since he had experienced any concern for his well being. He was superstitious about such things and just at this moment, he felt that a rebuff to any kindness, however small, might mean the last of any kindness at all.

So, he settled down with her and as he placed a nervous hand on her belly and as they were the only two people in this empty, moonlit world, he decided that this WOULD be his Margaret for as long as the sun kept its distance.

"What a pair we are," said Lesley drowsily.

"A couple of Lipton's orphans," Driscoll replied with a yawn. Lesley laughed. "The Start Rite Kids before they started."

Driscoll, more out of tenderness than anything else, tremulously reached out to encompass one small breast with his hand. He need not have worried for she was already fast asleep.

Sometime in the early hours of the morning he was awoken by Lesley massaging his chest, moving her hand round and round in circles and working her way lower and lower. He opened bleary eyes to see her smiling down at him. She looked younger than she had previously but even more vulnerable.

He put his hand over hers and she stopped what she was doing to look down at him quizzically.

"What's the matter?" she asked in a voice husky with sleep.

He was groping for the appropriate words when, once again, he decided against rebuffing kindness. What if something like this never happened again in his whole life. He removed his hand from hers. She continued.

Once the Old Ceremony was over they lay exhausted in each other's arms. Driscoll glowed. He had just been brought out of the shadows again. Now he was more than just a memory in other people's lives. He was, however briefly, part of someone's life but, just to reassure himself that it was all real, he placed the tip of his finger under her left breast. Yes, there *was* another heart beating alongside his in this newly blessed dark. Outside the full moon was still riding high and mighty in his night kingdom and the reborn Driscoll was safe – for now.

The two refugees from the day lay in bed bathed in moon-glow and talking of life in generalities as if they feared that being too specific about anything would somehow exile them from the comfort of this bed and force them back on to cold streets again. When the spell cast upon you matches your desires, you will do anything not to break it.

They commiserated with each other's sadnesses and offered each other clichéd advice for a future which Driscoll fervently hoped could be held at bay forever. He would have been only too happy for this moment, this very one, to be his past, present and future all rolled into one. He knew that all too soon that arrogant ball of fire and gas would come raging over the rooftops looking for him. It would peer into every nook and cranny, illuminating each shabby, misshapen thing that was better left to the shadows. Burdened by this knowledge, he struggled heroically to stay awake but sleep overtook him.

He woke just after dawn, hoping for a last embrace to send him out into his solitary future, but he was already alone in his tainted bed. A noise by the door made him look up.

Lesley was slipping his wallet back into his inside jacket pocket. She saw him observing her with his old familiar, unkind eyes but she displayed no sign of fear or a guilty conscience as she held up three ten pound notes, splayed out like a fan. She was a business woman after all!

"That's fair, isn't it, sweetheart. I mean you had a good time, didn't you?"

12

SUNDAY MORNING ECHOES OF THE NIGHT BEFORE

Miss Laird had slept only fitfully through the night. By the morning it seemed to her that she had slept for no longer than an hour at any one time and this, she thought, was worse than not sleeping at all.

During her periods of wakefulness, which accounted for most of the night, the phone conversation repeated itself over and over and over again like a stuck record. She flushed with embarrassment that she had ever thought that Lachlan could have been interested in her in "that way".

What HAD she been thinking of, for goodness sake? Of all the silly schoolgirl nonsense. She would have hoped that Bill Todd had cured her of all that and she was sick with herself that she had not seemed to learn any lessons at all from that debacle – not even after all the pain that "sly Todd" had caused her.

She was supposed to be working hard to repair her fortunes after that "basket" had fleeced and jilted her – not jeopardising her current livelihood, for goodness sake. What a fool she had been. What would her dear mother make of all this?

At 8 a.m. Miss Laird decided to have a bath. There was always a chance that all those little imps responsible for her shame and self-loathing would shrivel up in the steam and never bother her again. Certainly, some of them succumbed as she wallowed in the hot bath water but enough survived to keep Elizabeth at least arm's length from peace of mind. Slowly, though, as the steam subsided, the sheer power of sour resentment came to her rescue.

Here she was, living in conditions which were little short of Dickensian, and yet she, and she alone, was the reason that Lachlan was making so much money out of that little hat shop in the West End. She was pretty sure too that it was one of his more profitable enterprises – apart from his flats anyway and, let's face it, she thought, dripping vinegar, any idiot could make money out of renting flats in Edinburgh these days. It didn't exactly take much imagination or flair. Certainly not as much as she needed to run that little shop which, by the way, regardless of what anyone thought, didn't run itself!

And you had to have an eye for colour and style – and price! Let's not forget about price. The whole thing was you had to be able to deal with people and that was never Lachlan's strong suit. Let's face it, he needed her more than she needed him if it came to that. She bit her lip and poisoned herself with her own venom.

A tear rolled down her cheek. She was making Lachlan a small fortune and getting peanuts back in return. The man couldn't even make a simple dinner arrangement and stick to it, for Pete's sake. It was hard not being appreciated. It was hard not to be the owner of your own success.

The tears were flowing freely now and as a veritable volcano of anger churned in her belly. She pounded the water with both fists. "Bloody Lachlan," she cried out loud. "Bloody Todd. Bloody threadbare carpets. Bloody tatty wallpaper."

She paused just long enough to catch her breath. "Bloody life. My bloody, bloody life!"

Somewhere, out of reach of the steam, a choir of imps were laughing themselves silly.

13

TEA AND EMPATHY

Miss Laird, head bowed in prayer, before the start of the Morning Service at St Mark's, asked her Maker if she might not be allowed a period of numbness – a sort of mental anaesthesia. She was reasonably confident of being able to deal properly with things after a brief respite but not just at the moment ... please, not just at the moment. Oh, if only the world would stop turning for a few hours!

Now she stood bathed in the light streaming through the acres of stained glass window and hoping fervently that she would be touched by some of the spray from The Asperges Twig as the Provost passed down the aisle.

He passed by and she felt nothing on cheek or hand but, before the seeds of disappointment could germinate fully within her, she noticed a drop of water on her Order of Service and she gazed at it intently for a moment while fighting back the ungracious thought that it was, after all, only a consolation prize. As usual something good had only come to her indirectly and incompletely.

After the Service she decided to forego the usual tea and biscuits in the vestry. She was in no mood for idle chit chat or the clichéd every day pleasantries. She was on a short fuse and she had no desire to say anything that she might regret next Sunday. Church life had always been important to her and she had the feeling that it would be even more so in the days to come.

She slipped away with barely a nod to anyone and headed back in the direction of her bedsit but, not exactly being eager to get back to "that Mausoleum", her stride was not its usual vigorous and confident self.

As she passed the gates of the Botanic Gardens the brush of an April zephyr on her cheek made her suddenly aware of the world around her. She stopped and turned in the direction of the Gardens. The beauty of this Spring day tugged at her heart.

Well, there was an idea, she thought. She could have her cuppa after all in the Gardens Tea Room and then idle away the afternoon pleasantly enough looking at green and hopeful things. About twenty minutes later Buster bowled confidently through the same gate. He had no need of help from any passing Spring breeze. He was here on duty. He had a mission to fulfil. There were squirrels to feed.

Miss Laird could not deny a small pang of melancholy as she sipped her tea for, all around her, in the Botanic Garden Tea Rooms were couples and parents with children and yet here she was, another Spring and still on her own and still at No. 17.

She was supposed to be enjoying a different life by now but circumstances had forced her far from the course set by herself and, instead of blaming the metaphorical reefs that lay just under life's surface and on which she had certainly come to grief not a few times recently, she did that typical Scots Calvinist thing and blamed herself instead. It was all her fault. She should have seen things coming. She should have listened to her mother. She should most certainly have smelt a rat with the Todd thing.

Her siblings had satisfactory and even spectacular lives. Why couldn't she?

To be honest she wasn't quite sure in what way her life should be different but she was quite sure that it would not involve stale-smelling rooms, threadbare carpets and strange fellow lodgers.

Lodgers! How she hated that word. Surely, if any single word in the English language conjured up the idea of failure – it was "Lodger". It spoke so richly of failed, unresolved lives ... of impermanence and, most of all, of low status.

This alternate life, only ever seen through the mists of wishful thinking, would not have involved being alone either. She took a deep breath, as though hoping that it would flush these morbid thoughts out of her system and, after another sip of tea, she turned her mind back to the morning's sermon. Yes, indeed, despair was a sin – and it was also very tiring.

A little girl in a red matinee coat stood a few feet away studying her with the intentness of those for whom the world is still a minute by minute adventure.

"Hello, poppet," said Miss Laird, glad of the distraction. "What's your name?"

The child laughed and hid her face behind her hands and, for the first time since Lachlan's call, Elizabeth Laird, 42 and still spinster of this parish, smiled too.

She was still smiling when she happened to glance over in the direction of the self-service counter in time to see Buster staring back at her, mouth opening and shutting, like a terrified goldfish. Miss Laird's smile vanished like snow on a griddle and Buster vanished, as best he could, behind a portly lady just ahead of him in the queue.

He had only come in to the tea room because he had not realised that he had forgotten, in his haste to get out of the horrible dark house and into the sunlight, that he had nothing to give the curly tailed ones. Besides, he was feeling rather peckish himself and it was always good if you could kill two birds with one stone. It seemed to him, though, a bit thick that, so often when you tried to do a good deed for others, you landed up in the soup yourself.

Now he just wanted to get the things he had come in for and to get away sharpish. He certainly didn't want any more trouble. So far, Edinburgh seemed to have had more trouble in store for him than he was used to in a whole year and he'd only been here a few days!

It was bad enough to get a dressing-down when you were the only one in the room but it would be a thousand times worse if the mad lady lost her rag in front of all those people. Just as he was reflecting on what form his humiliation might take this time, the portly lady was served and his cover had gone.

"Yes, dear?" said the motherly woman at the counter.

Buster shot Miss Laird a nervous glance before giving the counter lady his order along with a polite request that she place the items in two separate paper bags.

Whether it was to do with the Reverend Mackie's sermon, or the strain of holding on to bitterness for too long, Miss Laird did not know but she found that her anger towards this unfortunate "bathroom hogger" had

TEA AND EMPATHY

completely leeched away and she was now wondering what the "poor soul" was doing wandering about without any supervision.

Buster grinned nervously as the woman behind the counter made a great pantomime of putting ginger biscuits and Dundee Cake into the two paper bags. She was well meaning but he just wished that she would *GET ON WITH IT!*

At last, Buster got the chance to pay for his purchases just as Miss Laird rose from her chair in that semi – automatic way that people do at religious rallies. She had to get this off her chest and she would make a start by buying this eccentric lodger a cup of tea and taking the opportunity to tell him how sorry she was for her unkindness. She took a few steps toward Buster, her face etched with a mixture of contrition and concern. Unfortunately for her, he turned from the counter just in time to see the "mad lady" bearing down on him and he, not being the most skilled at reading facial expressions, thought that his worst fears had been confirmed and that he was about to be read the Riot Act again.

Once more he fled from Miss Laird's clutches, leaving her standing, open – mouthed, in the middle of the tea room. Suddenly the poor woman was aware of many, many pairs of eyes burning into her back. She slipped back to her table, picked up her handbag and scuttled out, mortified.

14

LOVED AND UNLOVED

Buster made several attempts at reading an old magazine that some previous inhabitant had left in his room but he could not get much beyond the second paragraph of any of its articles.

He paced back and forth across the worn carpet. He hummed and hawed and rolled his eyeballs in theatrical exaggeration.

He stared forlornly out of the window like a fat, bald Rapunzel waiting for a rescuer. He flounced down on the bed and its springs registered their distress loudly and then he closed his eyes and wished that he could doze away the couple of hours until his next meal was due. It was no use though. He could not even settle to dozing.

The splendours of that wonderful Garden had spoiled him for this gloomy place. The memory of all that Spring light and colour rebuked the shadows between these four walls, but outside the sky was still blue and the clouds scudding across it were still as big and fleecy and, suddenly, Buster could stand this confinement no longer.

He grabbed his coat, for it was still only Spring in Edinburgh, and his little, blue transistor radio, and rejoiced at the sound of his room door slamming shut behind him.

Outside the April breeze was still fresh in the street and he sat down on the doorstep and turned on his radio.

Across the street a cat dozed on top of a wall. Buster wondered, idly, if it was his acquaintance of the previous evening and thought it might be nice to go over and stroke it, but then he thought better of the idea. Cats had to get their forty winks where they could. They were up all night after all.

In the living room just behind Buster, the old landlord was drifting in and out of sleep and between his two worlds. He could hear music coming from that beloved older world which, as the years marched on, he found easier and easier to return to.

He knew the music well. It was fiddle music. Wedding music. Strangely, though, he was beginning to hear it even when he was certain that he was awake.

"Surely not," he murmured to himself. This was wedding music and it belonged only to that other time and it made him think of his bride, now far beyond the shadows, and he "looked" on her again with all the love of a young bridegroom.

The fiddle music got louder.

"Surely not." He yawned and rubbed his eyes. He was awake. He was. He knew he was. It was real music and no dream, but where was it coming from?

Josef raised himself unsteadily on to his feet, too impatient for an answer to bother looking for his walking stick and staggered over to the window.

He laughed when he saw the scene outside. He could not help himself. His eccentric little guest just seemed to have that effect on him. The Greeks had a word for this phenomenon – or was it the Romans? It didn't much matter. He grinned like a village idiot as he watched Buster with the little blue radio clapped to his ear, swaying back and forth in time to the fiddle music.

Josef tapped on the window.

There were tea and cakes as before. And shortbread. There were the old man's memories and the gallery of family and friends looking out from their silver frames, all as before.

This time, though, Buster had already been introduced to them and so, by his lights, they were now his friends too. After tea and cake, when the old man had momentarily tired of talking, and lay back in his chair staring at the ceiling, Buster thought that it would be nice to reacquaint himself with all the faces in the frames.

He worked along the line of photographs until he came to one of a delicately featured young woman whose mass of black curls spilled out from under her wedding head dress. Buster fell in love instantly. He clasped the picture to his bosom and stared soulfully out of the window and up to the blue infinite. His emotions were too overwhelming to be constrained by this room.

The old man studied him with an indulgent smile. He did not begrudge the little man his moment. He was not in the least offended by Buster's handling of the photograph. The little simpleton meant no offence. He had no malice in him.

When, at last, Buster had composed himself, he crossed the room and reverently placed the photograph in the old man's lap. Josef looked at the long-lost bride for whose benefit the music had been and then at Buster, whose eyes were now great pools of unspoken questions, and motioned him to sit down.

The old man knew how to tell a story all right. His words may have been halting and barely audible but they soon began to work their magic on his guest who sat with his hands folded on his lap, his eyes tight shut and a beatific smile plastered across his silly face.

Josef's words swirled around him and quickly burrowed deep into his consciousness and deeper and deeper and before very long, the old man's words became vision in Buster's minds eye and, before much longer, concentrating hard with eyes still screwed tight shut, he could feel the room of that long ago celebration all around him and smell the wedding flowers and feel the presence of the very guests at the wedding meal.

He knew only too well that he could stay amongst this gathering just as long as he remembered to keep his eyes shut and for as long as the old man kept on talking.

Now he fancied that he was walking the length of the banqueting table that was set with a cloth of the finest white lace and filled with candle light that danced across the silver table ware and recorded its glow in the faces of the guests who turned to smile at him as he passed the backs of their chairs.

There were no uniforms here. No one was shouting at him or chasing him away. No one was nudging their neighbour or sniggering. He did not feel like a stranger here – or a nuisance.

Near the head of the table, where the bride and groom sat, there was an empty place. It seemed to be for him. He sat down, bowing and smiling. Looking down at his plate, he noticed there was some unfamiliar delicacy set before him and also a glass of wine, the colour of rubies, to hand and for a brief moment, he was beguiled by the effect of the candle light on the colour of the wine, but for once in his life, it was not the food or drink that interested him.

When he looked up from the table the first gaze that met his was that of the bride. Black curls peaked out from under her head dress, just as they had in the photograph, but now here she was in the flesh and almost close enough to touch and she was regarding Buster with the sort of affectionate expression appropriate for a much-loved friend on a happy occasion such as this.

Buster was very sure that he had done nothing to deserve all this attention and looked away, embarrassed, but her gaze drew him back and her smile melted all his awkwardness and soon it felt as though his tired old skin had melted away too, to be replaced by a new one that would serve to protect him from all the vicissitudes that life might throw his way.

If people laughed at him in the future what of it? If they shouted at him or scowled or were cruel with their tongues … well none of that would penetrate this new skin, would it?

He felt completely at ease in this new skin. The weariness of all his travels, all the miles and the strange places and the different rooms and all the rainy days and cold nights and loneliness that lay behind him slipped from his shoulders. Oh, if only he could stay here forever. If there were no more cold station platforms, or strange beds or unfriendly faces would that not be ... heaven.

His eyes were still tight shut and somewhere in the background he could still hear Josef's voice. The air in this world was heavy with the scent of roses and velvet with the glow of candlelight and ringing with the sound of laughter and, when he dared to look again, the bride was still smiling at him from under her cascade of black curls and Buster smiled back at her, lost, for the moment, to the cold and real world beyond this room.

But, just at the summit of his happiness, the bride's smile started to fade and the features of her face seemed to move around in front of his eyes and, try as he might, he could not will them to reorder them selves and it was then that he realised that he could not hear the old man's voice any more.

When Buster opened his eyes again he saw that the landlord was fast asleep in the big leather armchair. The room was silent and the music and laughter from that other world which, at this moment, still seemed much more real to Buster, had gone itself to silence.

He lifted the framed photograph from the old man's lap and put it back in the spot where he had found it. Then, one by one, he bade farewell to all the other faces in all the other photographs and left the old man to his dreams.

LOVED AND UNLOVED

As he climbed the stairs Buster envied his friend, for the old man could return to that world any time that he wanted to, but he himself, would have to be invited.

15

THE HIGH PRICE OF CHIPS

At 6 p.m. sharp, Miss Laird kicked off her shoes and sat down to enjoy *Your Hundred Best Tunes* on the wireless, as she still insisted on calling it.

The Autumn Leaves and *Moon River* worked their magic as they soothed her qualms about seeing Lachlan face to face at the start of the working week but, half way through *The Very Thought Of You*, her reverie was interrupted by a wild yell from the kitchenette next door, followed by what sounded like a baby elephant running back and forth along the landing outside her door and a shrill hysterical voice shouting "Danger", "Help" and "S.O.S." in strict rotation.

Miss Laird, who had been hovering on the edge of sleep, shook herself awake and tried to make sense of the din but, before she could do so, there was a mighty hammering on the door of her room.

Buster was babbling away at her even before she had a chance to open the door. Reading between the lines, she learned that he had tried to cook some chips, forgetting to get rid of the excess moisture before he had thrown them into the pan of hot oil with the inevitable result. Still in something of a daze, she let him lead her to the kitchen door.

Miss Laird had a life long terror of fire. She had seen all the Government safety adverts that she had ever wanted to about chip pan fires and the mayhem that they could cause. She had been appalled to learn that nearly fifty per cent of all domestic conflagrations started because some greedy beggar wanted chips with it!

At the kitchen door Miss Laird froze. What had, a few minutes before, been a kitchen implement was now the base of a blazing inferno. "Oh sweet heaven!" she said to no-one in particular.

She was aware of Buster, the greedy beggar in question, squeezing her hand. She looked down at him. His shocked remorseful eyes were big enough to drown in. They pleaded with her silently but eloquently to pleeeeeeeeeze find a way to deliver this house and its occupants from the peril he had placed them in. Miss Laird fancied she could hear a thundering heartbeat and was not sure whether it was hers or his but, either way, a wave of pity washed over her.

She put her hand on his shoulder and said gently, but with some urgency, "Go and tell Mr. Straczyinski that there is a fire in the upstairs kitchen. Hurry, now!"

Buster looked doubtful.

"You don't have to tell him you started it, just go."

Buster took off down the stairs like a scalded cat. He was no longer an arsonist. He was a fireman now.

At the very moment he was banging on Josef's door, Elizabeth was gingerly attempting to move the chip pan from a curtain, at whose hem the fire was already licking, and on to another hob where it was not in contact with anything flammable. It was as much as she dared do for, even with her head held as far back as physically possible, she could still feel the heat clawing at her face and a brief, but terrifying, vision of herself with hair on fire passed before her eyes.

Remembering that damp towels were the thing required by this sort of situation, she looked around for one but after finding it, she forgot, in her state of panic, to wet it with the inevitable result that the fire devoured the dish towel in a couple of seconds and then somehow the other curtain was ablaze. Before long the smoke that was building up in the small room was beginning to catch at Elizabeth's throat and she feared that the thing was beyond her already, and she could no longer keep her terror in check and so she beat a retreat, closing the kitchen door firmly behind her.

On the landing she felt a spasm of shame at her cowardice but now it was as if some trigger had been pulled inside her, catapulting her into muscular, decisive action. She ran along to Driscoll's door and thumped on it with the heel of her hand shouting, "Fire. Fire. Get out. Get out." And felt very foolish when it was obvious that he wasn't in.

Then she raced down the half-lit stairway at break neck speed awed by this new strange state that she found herself in. Nothing seemed to matter anymore: not her job, not Lachlan, not even her recent humiliation. Nothing mattered except making sure that every living soul got out of the house in one piece.

She barged in to the old man's room and found him sitting in his leather armchair, phone in hand, trying to tell the emergency services operator what she needed to know, but it was obvious from Josef's facial contortions that he was having the greatest of difficulties in making himself understood, and all the time Buster stood at his side covering his eyes and shifting from one foot to the other in his agitation.

Miss Laird held out her hand and Josef obediently handed her the receiver. She was surprised, given the circumstances, at how cool and authoritative she managed to sound.

"Yes, I'd like to report a chip pan fire at No. 17 Stockwell Street. I really did try to put it out but I am afraid that it's beyond me now. Yes, I understand. No, I won't. Thank you."

Only then was there a hint of panic in her voice. "But hurry, please."

The old man allowed himself a thin smile of relief. Miss Laird, the efficient business lady who he had always admired and respected, was in charge. Everything would be fine now. No need for worry. He had seen worse things than this, after all. Buster stood still now and took his hands from his eyes and beamed at them both. The mad lady would lead them all out of their current predicament – he had already forgotten that he was the cause of it – and all would be well. He took a step forward and patted her gingerly on the shoulder in admiration.

Miss Laird, however, was oblivious to this tribute. Her mind was on her next move. She had remembered the old black Daimler parked on the other side of the road. All the time that she had been living at No. 17 she had never seen it move from that spot but, now and then, when she had either been coming or going, she had seen the old fellow sitting behind the wheel and staring out through the windscreen as if he was looking down some long road to a happier past.

Well, at least these two would be safe enough there for the time being, she reasoned and, grabbing his heavy woollen coat from the peg on the back of his door, she bundled the old man and Buster out of the house, across the road and into the back seat of the Daimler and then settled herself in front behind the wheel.

Nothing to do now until the Fire Brigade arrived, she mused out loud, running her hands admiringly over the walnut fascia.

"This IS a lovely car, Mr Straczyinski." She could sense him beaming with pride behind her. She looked at her watch, squinting to read the face in the glow of the street light. Probably about five minutes since she had phoned, she reckoned, not much more. Time was a funny thing. In the house it had flown and now …

She was suddenly aware of the pressure of silence and looked around to check on her two "charges" and found herself not knowing whether to laugh or cry. In the half light, sitting side by side, they looked, for all the world, like a pair of comic puppets left on the shelf long ago by some child grown too old to appreciate their strangeness.

Josef studied Elizabeth's face for a long moment before leaning forward to whisper his concern for the photograph of his bride.

She feared he might be in shock so, laying her hand on his, she said as gently as she could, "No, darling, safer to stay here. The fire isn't in your room. I'm sure the Fire

Brigade will put the fire out long before it gets to your room."

It was no good, though. She could see his eyes moisten at the thought of this second destruction of the old world, whose memory had kept his body and soul together all those years. His hand trembled on the back of her seat and she knew that her logic was of no comfort to him.

Buster, who had been silent up till now, chose this moment to add his "fourpence worth". He sucked in his breath and poked Elizabeth's elbow with a fat forefinger and gabbled something about the lady in the wedding dress with black curls. Miss Laird shushed him impatiently but Josef, who heard everything, spoke the beloved's name and Buster repeated it reverently.

The silence and the sadness and the thought of the old man losing this memento was too much for Elizabeth. She turned to Buster with a steely glint in her eye.

"Keep your eye on Mr. Straczynski and stay in the car or ... heaven help you." Buster, who took the look in her eye as a hint of a returning madness, nodded vigorously.

The blaze still being confined to the floor above, gave her ample time to find the photograph and leave the house in safety but, just as she shut the door to Josef's room behind her, the very thing that killed the cat tugged at her sleeve.

She could not see much evidence of the fire from where she stood on the ground floor and, because of badly blocked sinuses, she could not smell smoke either. Terrified as she was of fire, she felt herself drawn closer and closer to it like a child steeling itself to see whether or not there really is a monster in the bedroom cupboard.

How far had the fire advanced? What else had it consumed by now? Would the rest of the house be saved?

As if under some malign hypnosis she started to climb the stairs, step by trembling step, stopping once, in a moment of sanity before daring herself to carry on, wanting to know all the answers to the aforementioned questions but terrified of finding out.

She could now see the kitchen door still firmly shut and remembered reading somewhere that if you shut the door on a fire it could buy you a little time. Then Buster's voice came crashing through her trance.

She was about to give him a telling – off for disobeying her but she turned too quickly, catching her heel in the ratty old stair carpet and, clawing uselessly at the air, she tumbled down the full length of the stairs.

If she made a bit of an effort she could just see the tree outside her window. It was a fine, sturdy oak. She thought, idly, that it would look wonderful in the Summer and more so in the Autumn.

She felt a happy surprise that she no longer seemed concerned about her future. Some of that was undoubtedly down to the painkillers but she knew it was more than that. Something had happened. Something was different. A door had been opened and she had been released from that horrible, sad little room and out into broad daylight. She could breathe again. Strange how one stupid accident could lead to so many wonderful things.

Another wave of dopeyness passed through her. Ooooh those painkillers were strong! The warm glow they gave was delicious – like taking a bath in warm chocolate – but then she started to feel as if she was floating and she did not think this was quite proper so she tried to fight the feeling by gripping the sides of the bed's mattress as tightly as she could.

This had the effect of letting her doubts come creeping back. Lachlan hadn't been in to see her after all, had he? She had imagined the whole blessed thing. He hadn't offered to put her up rent free indefinitely as a belated token of his gratitude for all that she had done for his business. He wasn't going to look after her. She was nothing to him.

Her eyes moistened and prickled. She felt all the recently gained warmth and security and the first hint of happiness draining away like Spring rain into the soil. She felt an overwhelming tiredness. She closed her eyes and relaxed her grip on the mattress. She surrendered. Floating away was not to be feared any more. She wanted to float away.

The funny little man in the tatty raincoat and the hobnailed boots handed her the balloons with a smile. They were all different colours and her nine-year-old self thought that they were wonderful as they bobbed about in the bright air. She looked up at them open mouthed and spell bound but soon the balloons began to tug at her hand. She gripped them ever more tightly but the balloons tugged harder and harder as if they wanted to be free of her.

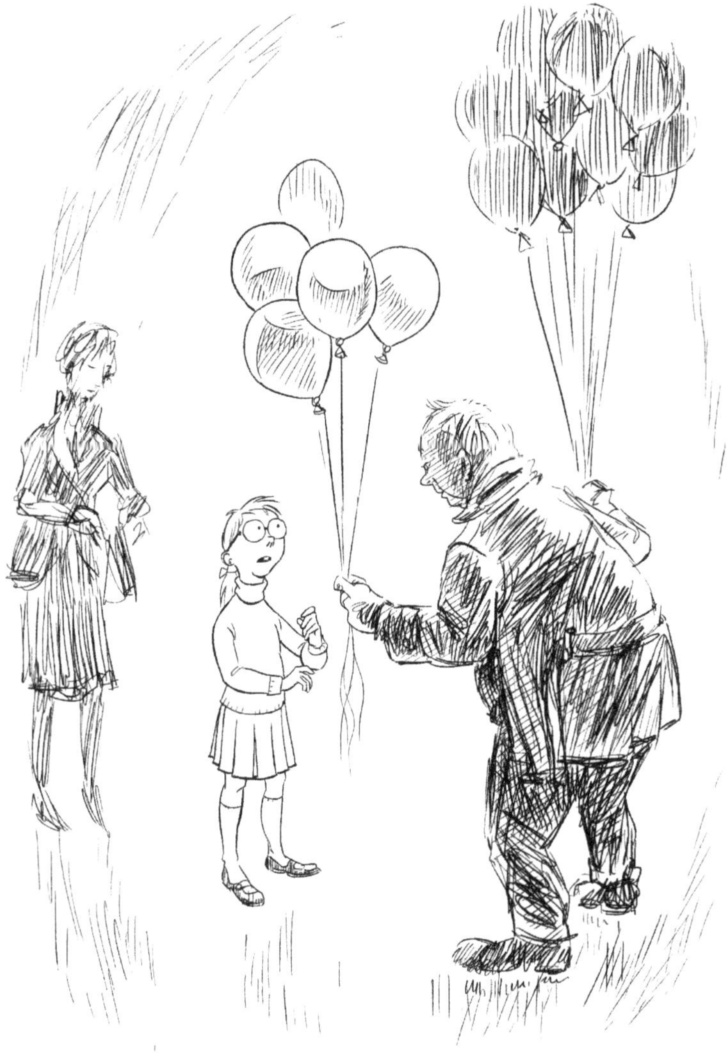

THE SCATTERING WINDS OF SPRING

She looked over to the Balloon Man for some sort of reassurance that all that colour and light would always belong to her, would always be within her grasp, but she could tell by his expression that she was meant to let go. She tried to hold on a little longer but it was no use. As her hand unfurled and the balloons drifted upward the little man smiled and nodded at the tearful child and she knew she had done the right thing and the tears stopped.

He was right. The shabby little man was right. He must have been for clearly he was happy too and the face that shone back at her in her half-dream was one that could only belong to a soul at peace with itself.

She drifted upwards herself now as free as those precious balloons and a peace as gentle as it was great came to claim her.

The old man lay in a ward at the other end of the hospital, a small creature adrift in a sea of white, dreaming with eyes wide open. Now the future was no longer a threat to the past and as he dreamed the long afternoon away, the ghost of a smile was just visible above the covers.

The sound of laughter and music on the other side of the door confused him at first but then a slow, sure understanding flowed through his entire being. Unafraid, heart rejoicing, he opened the door and entered.

Driscoll lay propped up on his bed lighting up another cigarette almost before he had stubbed out the previous one. He had reluctantly come to the conclusion that his recent encounter was some sort of supernatural visitation and an implied judgement on the cruelty of his younger self. He tried to work out the "whys and the wherefores" but the judgement just made his head spin and he started to cast around for distractions to keep his "ghost" at bay.

He was not having much success. The radio was no help. It was tuned in to one of those programmes where husbands request songs for wives that "mean the whole world to me" and wives compliment husbands on being "loving and caring and a wonderful father to our three smashing kids". Sons put Mothers on pedestals and Dads doted on daughters.

Driscoll sniffed and sneered at every mention of filial devotion and the witterings of uxorious husbands. Eventually, it was all too much for him and he switched the thing off with such force that the knob almost came off in his hands. It was understandable. No-one likes to be reminded of the things that life is denying them, still less to be reminded that they did once have those things but had thrown them away as if they were of no consequence whatsoever.

He sighed at the thought of his predicament. There was no doubt about it. It all kept coming back to the money. If it had only been enough to keep him bowling along for another couple of weeks things would have been simpler. It would have been easy enough to find another no hoper and put the whole bundle on that. The plan wouldn't have failed a second time. Not even a haunted embezzler could be that unlucky – surely!

6
THE SCATTERING WINDS OF SPRING

After the chip pan fire the house had more people coming and going than in the whole of the previous decade. Joseph's nephew had called to say that the house would be closed while repairs were carried out and until it was decided whether it would be sold or not.

Officials from the Fire Brigade were picking over the remains of the kitchen and a couple of police officers had shown up seeking a few words with Buster, but he had instinctively made himself scarce.

One sniff of a police uniform and Driscoll had dropped all thoughts of atonement like a hot potato. Atonement was all very well if the backside was hanging out of your trousers and you had nowhere else to go anyway. Let's face it, atonement was mandatory in a situation like that but, if you had options, well then, you had options.

Right now, Driscoll's main concern was one of logistics. In short, how was he going to hump all that money around securely? He had only one account that he was sure that the authorities did not know about but he could not deposit too much cash into it at any one time or certain people might get suspicious.

Suddenly, an idea occurred to him. If he bought some smart new togs up in town he could book into that "Fancy Dan" hotel at the end of Princes Street and hand them one of those smart leather zipper bags, with the padlocks, stuffed with cash and they'd obligingly bung it in their safe for him, same as they did for all the other toffs and that would give him some time to ponder his escape from Edinburgh. The Law would never think of looking for some-one like him in a place like that and he felt a certain sense of self justification in the thought that there would be far bigger crooks than him passing through the lobby of that particular hotel every hour of the day.

Buster sat on the bench at the top of the hill in his beloved Botanic Gardens, studying the view in front of him in minute detail. He took in every tree, every bush and bed of flowers in a grand attempt to commit it all to memory. He knew that some day, when he was "down in the dumps", he would want to remember what he could see before him now.

The world had turned again and there was nothing that he could do about it. A few short hours ago he had had nothing to worry about. He had been having an adventure in Spring in a strange city but now everything had changed. He had made a mess of things again. He hadn't meant to. He never did.

It didn't matter though. Now people would be angry with him and shout at him if they caught up with him and people in uniform would have a part in it somewhere. You could be sure of that. They might even put him in jail. You just never knew about these things.

Just as Buster was shivering at this prospect he was aware of someone watching him. She was about three years old with long, curly hair and was dressed in a crimson matinee coat.

She laughed suddenly and Buster smiled. She put her hands over her eyes and peeked out from behind them, first to her right and then to her left.

Buster fumbled in his pocket for a boiled sweet and, purely by chance, pulled out one almost the very colour of her coat. Tickled by this coincidence, he held it out to her.

The child hesitated for a moment with her hand outstretched towards Buster's gift. Then she looked over her shoulder at her approaching mother who, deciding that the little man was harmless, nodded her approval.

As mother and child continued on their way, Buster suddenly felt cheered again. He took a deep breath, picked up his battered suitcase and strode off down the hill. He felt brave now and certain that the world would soon be turning his way again.

No sooner had Driscoll boarded the London train than it juddered into life. His heart jumped. A few more minutes and he would be free of Auld Reekie. There was nothing here for him now except a certain and lengthy incarceration.

He was just about to pull the door shut behind him when his heart jumped again. That wee fat eejit who had nearly set No 17 up was running for the train. He was red in the face and looking as if he was about to explode at any moment but he wasn't going to give up. Not him.

Driscoll's grip on the door handle tightened as Buster drew level and looked up pleadingly. The train started to pick up speed. Buster was drenched in sweat by now. He looked as if he was about to have a heart attack.

"Stupit wee bastard" muttered Driscoll before holding out his hand and, with every last ounce of strength at his disposal, yanking Buster and his suitcase aboard.

It had been a good week for Miss Laird – the first in her new position. The "new arrangement" was working very well.

At five o'clock she shut up shop and headed off to her "new" New Town flat. She was in no hurry. She was glad of the time to savour the pleasures of her new situation.

Lachlan would probably be out. He was out most nights. She marvelled at the brilliance of his social life. The people he knew!!!!!!! All those elegant and artistic young men. Actors. Antique dealers – all very glamorous. It was obviously what kept him so young.

She didn't mind being on her own in the flat. Her end of it was more or less self contained anyway and, although it was nice to chat to Lachlan over a coffee on one of those rare occasions when their paths met, she didn't feel lonely when he wasn't there. Besides, it was such a lovely flat, almost a companion in itself. And when he was there he always had so much to talk about. He was always fizzing with ideas. He was affectionate and solicitous too. He was a joy really.

Her new life was a joy. Her job was a joy and it would all continue to be a joy as long as she was a sensible girl and didn't ask for too much.

She remembered how it was when she was a little girl looking for shells along the beach. She would start out looking for something beautiful and ornate and exotic but, really, she would be happy enough with anything that caught her eye — even a piece of worn, green glass from some long-forgotten gin bottle thrown overboard far away.

She would pick up all these little gems and store them safely away. She did not want any of these small treasures ever to be lost. They would be there whenever she had need of them. In this way she could keep loneliness at bay forever.

*Available worldwide from Amazon
and all good bookstores*

Michael Terence Publishing

www.mtp.agency

mtp.agency

@mtp_agency